ALAN'S BIG, SCARY TEETH

THE FAMILY TREE

KING ALAN VI

ALANETTA

DR ALAN SMITH

FOR MY JENNA x

First published 2016 by Walker Books Ltd, 87 Vauxhall Walk, London SE11 5HJ

2 4 6 8 10 9 7 5 3 1

© 2016 Jarvis

The right of Jarvis to be identified as author/illustrator of this work has been
asserted by him in accordance with the Copyright, Designs and Patents Act 1988

This book has been typeset in Mrs Ant

Printed in China

British Library Cataloguing in Publication Data:
a catalogue record for this book is available from the British Library

ISBN 978-1-4063-6112-4 (hardback)
ISBN 978-1-4063-7080-5 (paperback)

www.walker.co.uk

ALAN'S BIG, SCARY TEETH

by
JARVIS

WALKER BOOKS
AND SUBSIDIARIES
LONDON · BOSTON · SYDNEY · AUCKLAND

Alan came from a long line
of very scary alligators.
He was known throughout
the jungle for his scaring.

It was what he did best.

Alan would start each day ...

polishing his scales,
sharpening his nails ...

and brushing each of his
big, scary teeth for
(at least) ten minutes
at a time.

SNAP SNAP
TOOTHPASTE

And after practising his
frightening faces in
the mirror ...

GRRR!

SNAP SNAP
TOOTHPASTE

SHINY SHINY POLISH

EAU DE
GATOR

And, "GRRR! GRRR!"

GRRR! GRRR!

He said things like, "I'M BIG, SCARY ALAN! FEAR MY RAZOR-SHARP TEETH!"

He made the frogs leap off their lily pads, the monkeys tumble from the trees and the parrots screech in terrible terror.

After a long day of scaring the jungle animals, Alan would head back home to the swamp, relax, finish the crossword in the *Jungle Times* and ...

TAKE OUT HIS FALSE TEETH!

NOBODY knew about
Alan's false teeth.

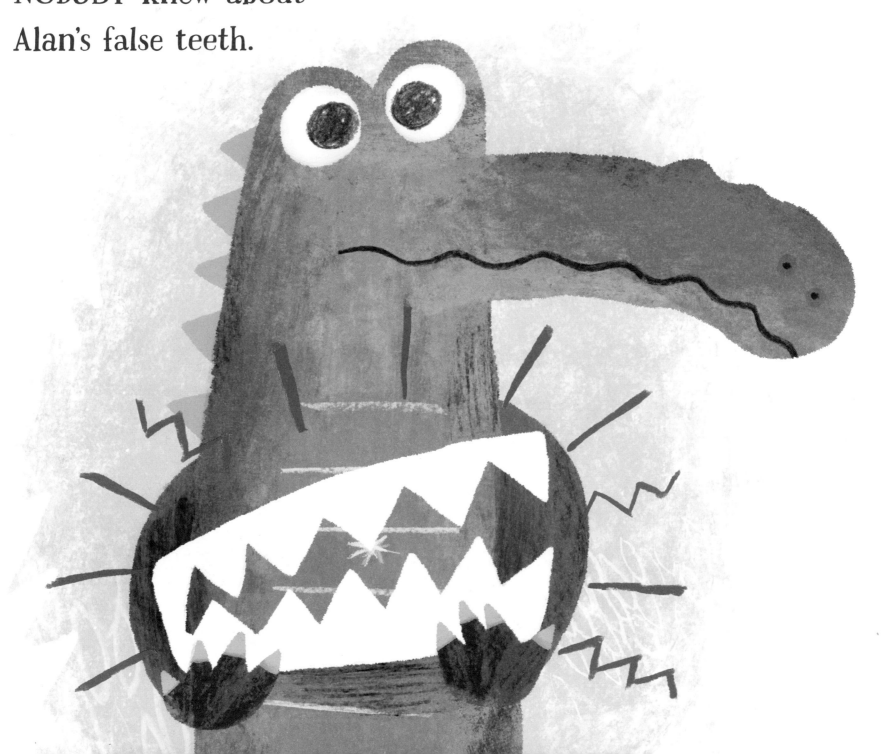

"Good night teeth. Thweet dweams my thcary thnappers," Alan would say, as he put them away carefully in his super-secret hiding place.

One morning, Barry the beaver was up
early collecting wood and came
across a dozing Alan.

Terrified that Alan might wake up and
gobble him whole, he quickly
dived behind a bush.

SNORT!
SNORT!

Phew! That was close, thought Barry, just as a set of false teeth fell out of a bush with a very familiar *"SNAP! SNAP!"*

SNAP! SNAP!

When Alan awoke his teeth were GONE.
"MY TEETH! MY TEETH! WHERE ARE MY TEETH!"

What could he do?

Maybe no one would notice?

Could he still be scary
without them? He decided to
head into the jungle as usual.

He made the frogs
leap off their lily pads,
the monkeys tumble
from the trees and
the parrots screech ...

WITH LAUGHTER!

Alan just wasn't very scary
without his teeth.

Alan slunk back to
the swamp.
He had never been
more embarrassed.

He came from a long
line of very scary
alligators. Scaring was
all he had ever known.

What would Alan
do now?

Poor Alan began to cry.
Just a bit at first...

WAAH!

But then the tears kept coming. He howled and yowled more than all the jungle babies put together.

And he could not stop crying until...

Next morning all the animals turned up at Alan's swamp with his big, scary teeth.

"We'll give you back your teeth," said Frog.

THE RULES

"W-WEALLY?" said Alan.

"On ONE condition," said Parrot. "You have to stop scaring us."

"But what will I do? I don't know how to do ANYTHING else!"

"We have an idea," said Frog.

And so every day,
after polishing his
scales, sharpening his
nails and brushing
his big, scary teeth,
Alan headed into
the jungle ...

and became ...
Alan, the
gardener ...

WELCOME
TO THE
JUNGLE

GREEN
FINGERS

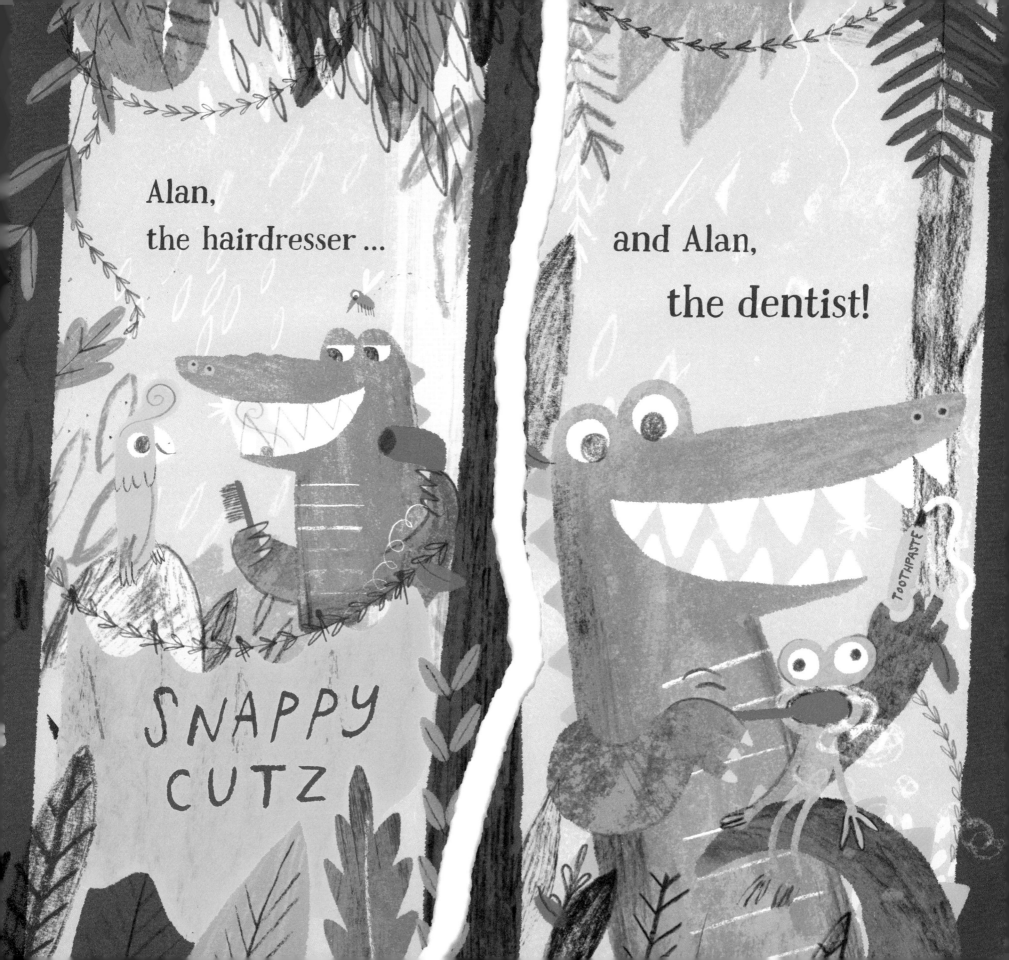

Alan, the hairdresser ...

and Alan, the dentist!

SNAPPY CUTZ

But every night ...
he became Alan the
BIG, SCARY STORYTELLER—
thrilling the jungle animals
with his terrifying tales.

"BWA-HA-HA!
I LOVE BEING SCARY,"
laughed Alan.

And sometimes...

he even let Barry borrow his teeth.

GRRR!